MW00954933

Oak Street TREEHOUSE

The Day The New Kid Moved In

Meet the friends at Oak Street Treehouse!

It was a cloudy Saturday afternoon at the treehouse. It was time for more games, books and of course chocolate chip cookies. Bandit and Buck were tugging on the same toy while Piper was snuggled up sound asleep against Cash. Cora was just walking in to join the treehouse fun.

Cora told everyone, “There is a moving truck across the street at the old Miller house. I miss when the Millers’ grandkids came to visit, and we got to play with them. They were so fun.”

Brit said, “Let’s go see the truck and find out who’s moving in.”

Annie wanted to finish reading, but everyone else went including Bandit and Buck. Piper snuggled up next to Annie.

MBozarth

OVE4U
THIS END UP
KITCHEN
FRAGILE
TOYS
MBozarth

The Oak Street kids were peeking over the bushes at the moving truck.

Addi said, “Two movers. It must be hard work! They are both sweating from lifting all the heavy furniture.”

Brit wanted to walk into the house and see what it looked like, but a car drove up and parked in the driveway.

C
MBozarth

Three people got out of the car.

Brit said, “I bet that is the dad, mom and their son.”

Cash said, “He looks like he’s your age, Brit.”

“He sure does have a lot of freckles!” Brit replied.

They heard the dad say, “Cooper, let’s go see what the house looks like and find your bedroom.”

Addi could hear the bell ringing at the front door of the treehouse. It was probably Annie letting them know that a warm, gooey batch of cookies had arrived.

When they stood up behind the bushes, the new kid, Cooper, saw them all. He waved, but no one took time to wave back. Cookies were more important at that moment.

Cooper asked his parents if he could go across the street to find out where all the kids went. Once around the bushes where the kids had been hiding, he could see the treehouse. Running over, he rang the bell and peeked inside the doorway. Piper woke up and started barking.

M Bozarth

Everyone was munching on cookies. Annie went to the door, hiding her cookie behind her back.

She said, "Hi, I'm Annie." Then everyone hid their cookies.

"Hi, I'm Cooper. We are just moving in across the street. This is a cool treehouse! Maybe I can come back and play once we are all moved in."

"Nice to meet you Cooper," Colt shouted from across the room. "Welcome to the Oak Street neighborhood."

Cooper answered, "Your dogs are cute. I've never had one. Well, I better go help my dad and mom. See ya all later I hope!"

He turned around and headed home.

It felt like everyone was thinking the same things:
Can't this just be OUR treehouse? We've been here since the treehouse was built Do we have to welcom EVERY new kid?

I wonder if God likes everybody? I don't want to SHARE our chocolate chip COOKIES!

It was so quiet you could have heard a cookie drop on the floor. That's when they heard the DING! on the tablet. Brit was in the middle of playing a game. She saw the message. It was from God!

Hi Oak Street Friends. I hope you are having a fun Saturday at the treehouse. I wondered when I would hear from you with another of your questions.

Your Friend, God

Colt walked over to their list of questions for God. He said, “I think we need to ask God question #4.” He read it out loud:

Do you really love everybody in the whole wide world?

Cora said, “It’s a good question for today since we have a new kid who wants to be part of the treehouse.”

Addi said, “His name is Cooper.”

Annie started to send the message to God.

“Ask God if we have to like people we’ve never met,” Cash said.

Brit added, “And do we have to let him in the treehouse too?”

DING!
Colt read the reply from God:
Dear God, do you really lov everybody in the whole wid world? Do we have to like people we don't know?
Oh, you met Cooper! And he wants to be part of the treehouse? And, you're not sure you want to let him join?
Yes, Oak Street Kids, I do love everyone in the whole world. One day I'll tell you how I showed everybody how much I love them. Cash, you show others you love them by including them whether they are nice to you or not...even strangers! Let me help you understand. Draw a picture of Cooper and put a blank paper on each side of the picture.

DING! Colt read the message from God:

On one page write the reasons you don't want to include him, and on the other sheet write all the reasons you might want him in the treehouse with you.

Cooper
Why we want to include him

DING! Colt read the message from God:

So you couldn't come up with any reasons to like Cooper?

Maybe it's because you don't even know him yet!

I have another idea. Addi, would you write these words down and tape the sheet on the wall: ***Sometimes the best gift you can give to someone is to include them.***

God

MBozarth

The kids talked about what God said...and that He really does love everyone in the whole world. They decided to walk over to the old Miller house. Now they call it the *Cooper* House. They brought a plate of chocolate chip cookies which were warm and gooey and as always, delish!

After introducing themselves to Cooper's dad and mom, they invited Cooper to come back to the treehouse and play.

Cash pushed Cooper as high as he could on the tire swing. All the girls were up in the crow's nest. When Cooper climbed up, they pointed out the pond across the street.

"There are worms, snakes and ducks - all sorts of cool things over there!" Brit told him.

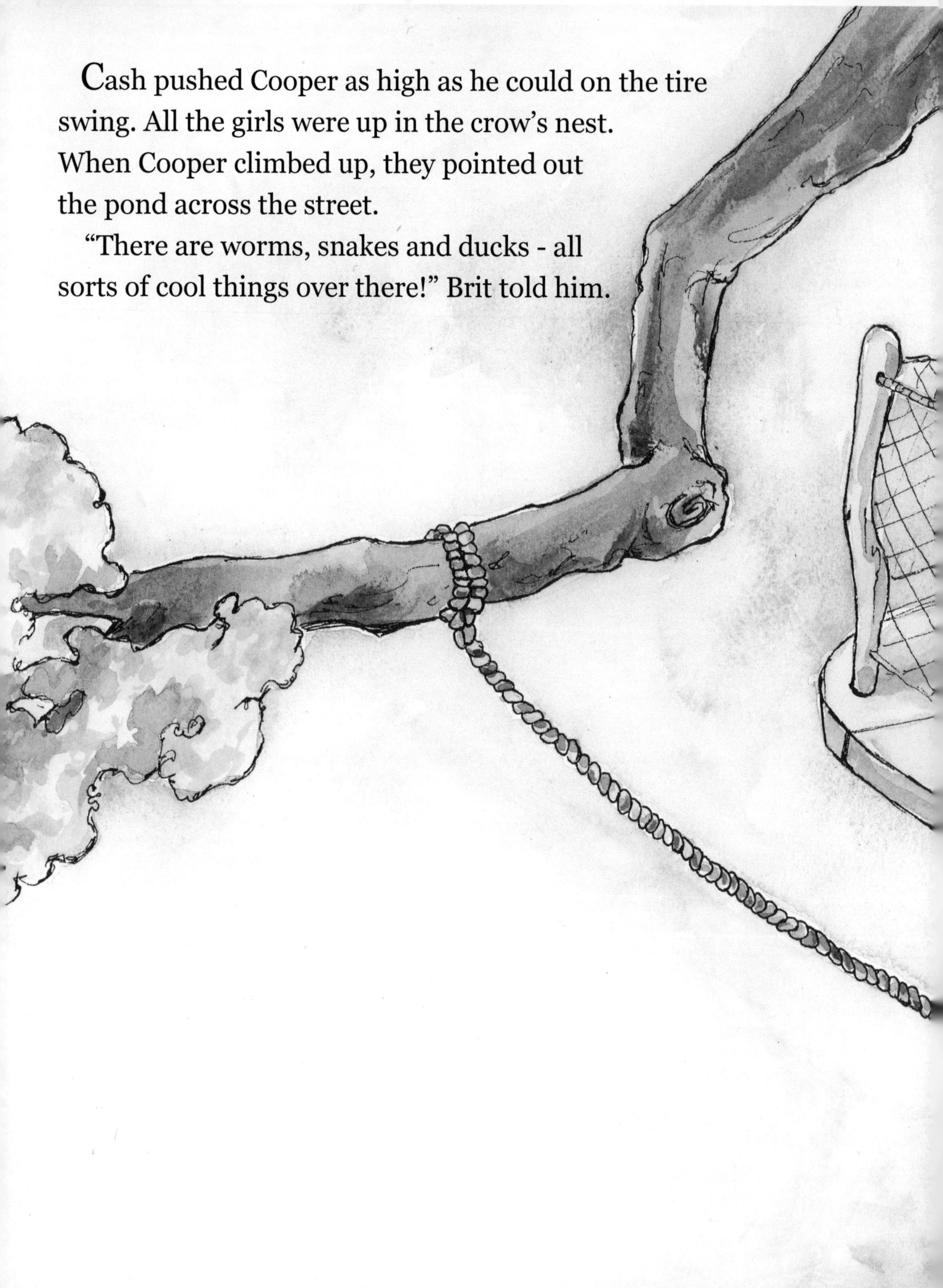

The kids gave Cooper a tour inside the treehouse. They showed him where they keep the cookies, the tablet for games, and treats for the dogs. He saw the list of questions for God and asked about it. Annie said everyone had to add one question to the list to be part of the Oak Street Treehouse.

Cooper added his question at the end of the list: *God, what happens when people die?*

Meet the friends at Oak Street Treehouse!

When Cooper asked about the quote on the wall, they all just looked at each other and started laughing!

They exclaimed, "Cooper, welcome to the Oak Street Treehouse!"

Written by Dick Daniels
Illustrated by Mollie Bozarth

Printed in the United States of America. Nashville, TN
Library of Congress Control Number: 2021913536
ISBN: 9781737081500

Meet the author and illustrator.

Dick was the new kid in fourth grade at a new school. It's never easy to break into existing networks of friends. Cooper is the new kid in this book. In real life he is cousin #7 to the rest of the Oak Street characters. Welcome to the Treehouse, Coop!

Dr. Dick Daniels is the President of The Leadership Development Group, including a LinkedIn Group of 30,000 global members.

www.theLDG.org

Mollie Bozarth remembers being the "new kid" at age 11 when her family moved from Virginia to Illinois. Some kids teased her about having a "southern" accent. But others stood up for her, making her feel welcomed. Those are friendships she'll never forget!

Mollie teaches high-school drawing and painting in Naperville, IL. She is a member of SCBWI (Society of Children's Book Writers & Illustrators) and Portrait Society of America.

molliebozarth.wordpress.com

Want more Oak Street fun? Check out OakStreetTreehouse.com for books, coloring pages, and discussion tips!

Printed in the USA
CPSIA information can be obtained
at www.ICGtesting.com
LVHW070003271023
761976LV00018B/408